WHAT DADDIES DO BEST

addies can teach you
how to ride a bicycle,

make a snowman with you,

and bake a delicious
cake for your birthday.

Daddies can help you
make a garden grow,

give you a
piggyback ride,

and take care of you
when you're sick.

Daddies can watch
the sun set with you,

sew the loose button
on your teddy bear,

and hold you when
you're feeling sad.

Daddies can take you
trick-or-treating,

help you give the
dog a bath,

and play with you
in the park.

Daddies can read you
a bedtime story,

tuck you in,

and kiss you good-night.

But best of all,
daddies can give you
lots and lots of love!

But best of all,
mommies can give you
lots and lots of love!

and kiss you good-night.

tuck you in,

Mommies can read you
a bedtime story,

and play with you
in the park.

help you give the
dog a bath,

Mommies can take you
trick-or-treating,

and hold you when
you're feeling sad.

sew the loose button
on your teddy bear,

Mommies can watch
the sun set with you,

and take care of you
when you're sick.

give you a
piggyback ride,

Mommies can help you
make a garden grow,

and bake a delicious
cake for your birthday.

make a snowman with you,

Mommies can teach you
how to ride a bicycle,

WHAT MOMMIES DO BEST

BY **Laura Numeroff**

ILLUSTRATED BY **Lynn Munsinger**

SCHOLASTIC INC.
New York   Toronto   London   Auckland   Sydney
Mexico City   New Delhi   Hong Kong